KU-765-540

Winnie AND Wilbur
AT THE SEASIDE

It was a very hot summer.
Winnie the Witch felt hot and tired.
Wilbur, her cat, felt hot and tired, too.
'I want a swim, Wilbur,' Winnie said.
'Let's go to the seaside.'

Winnie found her beach towel, her
beach bag and her beach umbrella.

VALERIE THOMAS AND KORKY PAUL

Winnie and Wilbur
SEASIDE ADVENTURES

Winnie and Wilbur AT THE SEASIDE

Winnie and Wilbur: THE PIRATE ADVENTURE

Winnie and Wilbur UNDER THE SEA

GREENWICH LIBRARIES

3 8028 02377557 7

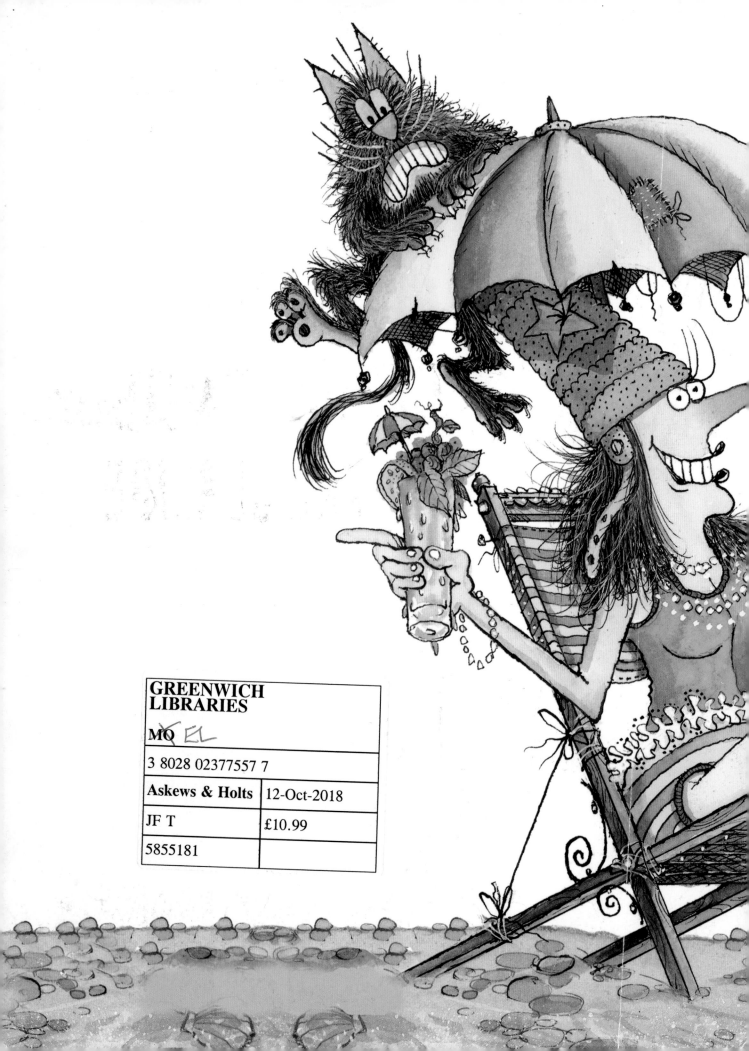

GREENWICH
LIBRARIES

MO EL

3 8028 02377557 7

Askews & Holts	12-Oct-2018
JF T	£10.99
5855181	

She jumped onto her broomstick,
Wilbur jumped onto her shoulder,
and they were off.

They flew over hot towns,
hot roads, hot cars,
and then they came to the sea.

There were lots of people on the beach,
but Winnie found a place for her towel.

She put up her beach umbrella
and got ready for her swim.

'Look after my bag and my broomstick, Wilbur,' Winnie said.
She ran into the water.

It was lovely in the sea.
Winnie splashed through the water,
and skipped over the little waves.
She was having a lovely time.

Wilbur sat and watched her.
He couldn't swim. He didn't like water.
He hated getting wet.

Winnie dived into the water. It was such fun!

But the water started to creep up the sand,
up to Winnie's towel.

Wilbur jumped onto
Winnie's beach umbrella.
'Meeow,' he cried.

Then the sea picked Winnie up, turned her over
three times, and dumped her on the sand.

The water washed over Winnie's towel,
and came half way up Winnie's beach bag.

'Meeeooooww,' cried Wilbur.
He didn't want to get wet.

'Oh dear,' said Winnie. She shook
some seaweed out of her hair.

'Don't worry, Wilbur.
We'll just move further up the beach.'

She picked up her beach bag and her towel.
'My broomstick!' cried Winnie. 'Where's my broomstick?'

She looked everywhere.

No broomstick.

Then she looked out to sea.
There was her broomstick, floating away.

'Stop!' Winnie shouted.
But her broomstick didn't stop.

'How will we get home, Wilbur?' cried Winnie.
Then she had an idea.
She grabbed her beach bag, took out her
magic wand, waved it five times, and shouted,

'Abracadabra!'

The broomstick stopped.

Then it started to come back.

But a surfer was in the way.

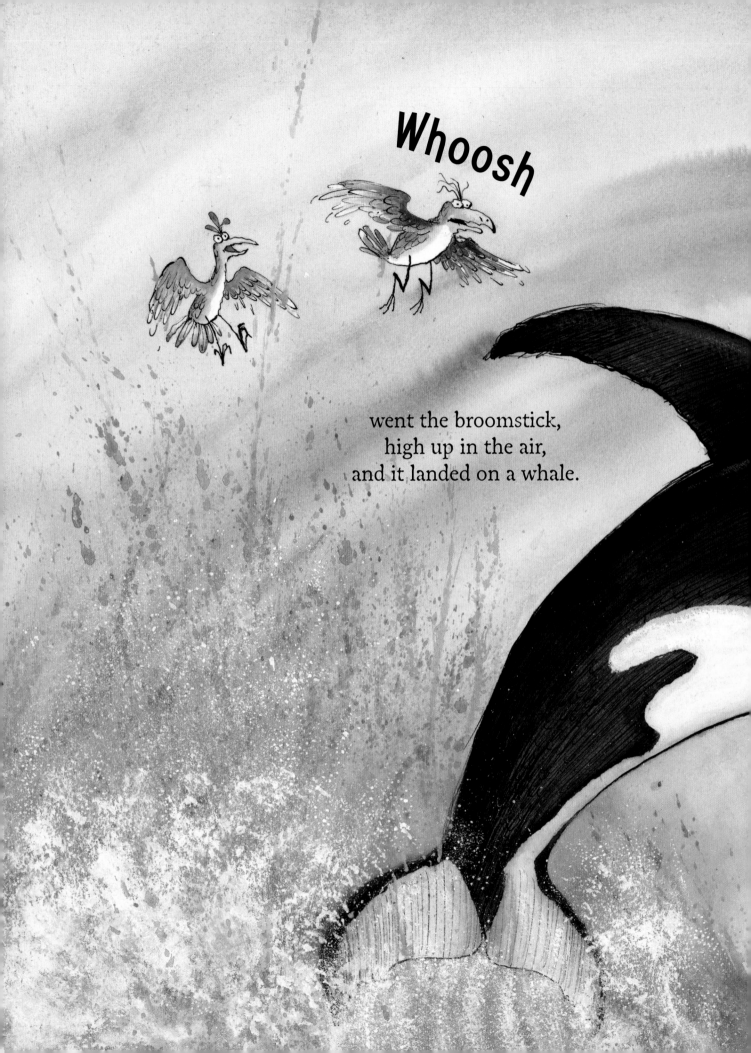

Whoosh

went the broomstick,
high up in the air,
and it landed on a whale.

The whale didn't want a broomstick on its back.

Whoosh

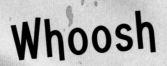

went the broomstick, high up in the air,
in a great spout of water.

Splash!

Winnie's broomstick had come back.
Winnie was pleased.

The other people on the beach
were not pleased at all.

They were very WET.

Wilbur was not pleased either.

He was very wet, very sandy,
and rather squashed.

'Oh dear,' Winnie said. 'We'd better go home, Wilbur.'
She packed everything up.

Then Winnie and Wilbur zoomed up into the sky.

They were soon home again.
It was still hot in Winnie's garden.
Winnie still felt hot and tired.

Then she had a wonderful idea.

She took her magic wand out of her beach bag,
shut her eyes, turned around three times,
and shouted,

'Abracadabra!'

There in her garden was
a beautiful swimming pool.

Winnie dived in.

She swam up and down, and
then she floated on her back.

'This is lovely, Wilbur,' she said.
'It's much nicer than the seaside.'

Anything is nicer than the seaside,
thought Wilbur.

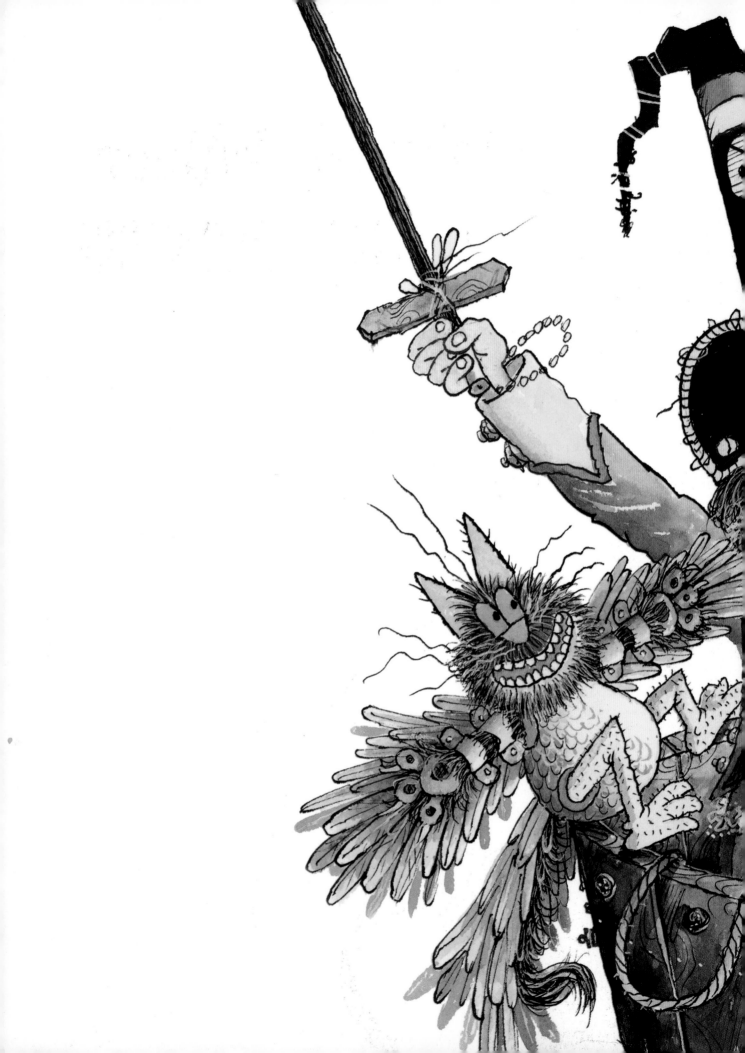

Winnie AND Wilbur
THE PIRATE ADVENTURE

Winnie the Witch and her big black cat
Wilbur were getting ready for a party.
It was a fancy dress party to celebrate
Cousin Cuthbert's birthday.

'What will we wear, Wilbur?' asked Winnie.
'We'll have to think about that.'

Winnie thought
about it.

Cinderella?
No.

. . . and there she was, wearing a pirate costume.
Wilbur was in a parrot suit.

Winnie was pleased.
'We look fantastic!' she said.

Wilbur was embarrassed.

We look ridiculous,
he thought.

Winnie jumped onto her broomstick,
Wilbur jumped onto her shoulder,
and they flew off to the party.

There were some wonderful
costumes at the party.

Fairies, clowns, a lion, a princess,
some spacemen and *lots* of pirates.

Happy Birthday, Cuthbert!

The other pirates admired Winnie's parrot.
Wilbur flapped his wings.

'All we need now is a treasure map,' one pirate said.
'I found a treasure map in my pocket,'
said another pirate.
'So all we need now is a ship.'

'I can do that,' said Winnie.
She waved her magic wand, shouted,

'Abracadabra!'

. . . and there was a pirate ship,
at the bottom of
Cuthbert's garden.

'Hurrah!'
shouted the pirates.
They climbed aboard
and sailed away.

'**Yo-ho-ho!**' shouted Winnie's pirates. 'Being a pirate is fun!'

They climbed up the masts.
They danced the hornpipe.
They walked the plank,
until Winnie fell in.

Luckily she could swim.

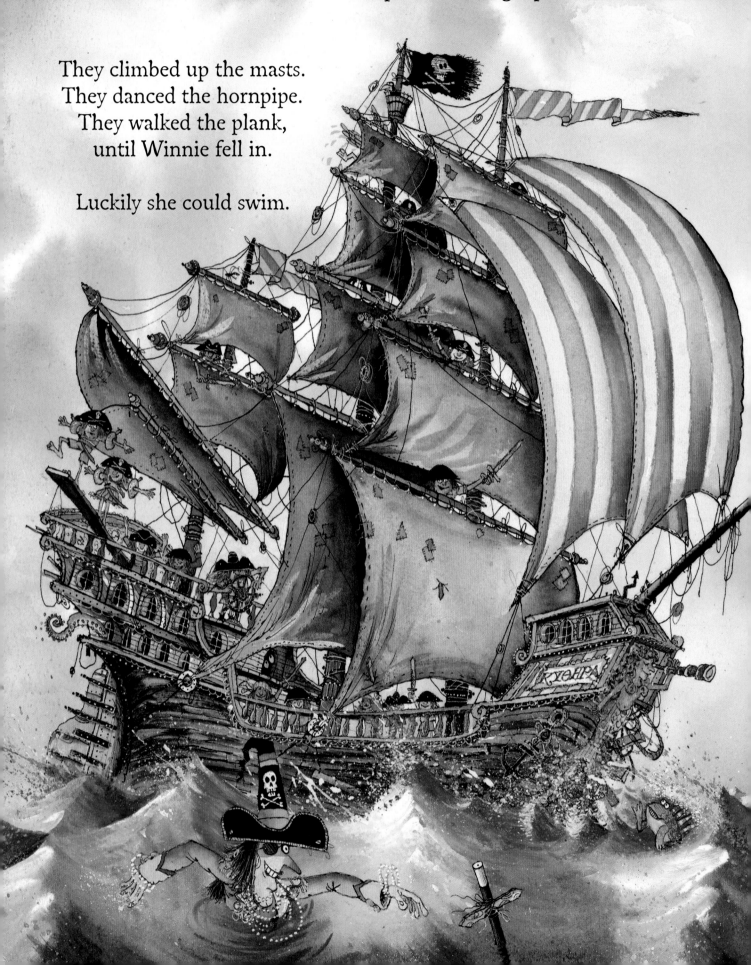

Wilbur climbed up to the crow's nest for a sleep,
but there was a crow inside.

'**Caw!**' said the crow.
She didn't want to share with a parrot.

Winnie's pirates got out the treasure map.
There were islands all around their ship.
Which one was the treasure island?

But then they saw an island
that looked exactly like the one
on the treasure map.

Winnie and her pirates splashed
ashore. They climbed to the top of a
hill and looked down.

There was another band of pirates digging up the treasure.
They had swords and daggers, cutlasses and blunderbusses.

They looked fierce.

'Will we stay and fight?' asked Winnie. 'Or go home?'

Winnie's pirates shouted . . .

'GO HOME!'

The real pirates looked up
and saw Winnie's pirates.

They ran back to their ship
with their swords and daggers,
their cutlasses and blunderbusses . . .

and sailed away.

Winnie's pirates were very surprised.

'Hurrah!' they shouted.
'We are fierce pirates!'

They ran down to the hole
in the sand and started digging.

It was hard work.

But at last they dug out the treasure chest.

Winnie lifted up the lid. The chest was empty.
'Shiver me timbers!' shouted Winnie's pirates.

'We've been hornswoggled!'

But Wilbur saw something
shining in the sand.

What was it?

He started to dig
and dig.

Out came a big shiny box.
And inside the box were lots
and lots of shiny tins . . . of sardines!

'Meee-yo-ho-ho!'
Wilbur was delighted. He loved sardines.

Winnie's pirates were not delighted.

But Winnie had a
wonderful idea.

She waved her wand,
shouted,

'Abracadabra!'

. . . and the
treasure chest
was full of
shiny treasure.

Now Winnie's pirates
were delighted.
They carried
the treasure and
Wilbur's sardines
back to the ship.

It was time to go home, but there was
no wind to blow their ship home again.

'I can fix that,' Winnie said.
She waved her magic wand,
and shouted, 'Abracadabra!'

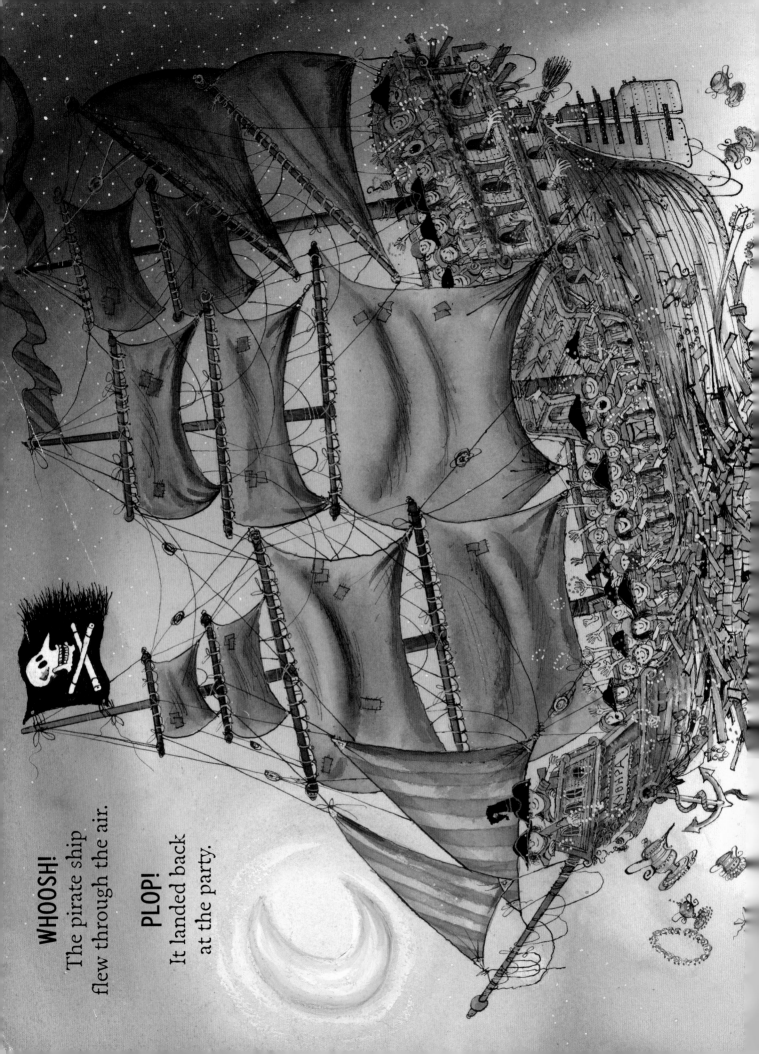

WHOOSH!
The pirate ship
flew through the air.

PLOP!
It landed back
at the party.

'Being a pirate is fun, Wilbur,'
Winnie said. 'But being a witch
is much more fun.'

'Purr, purr, purr,'
said Wilbur.

Winnie's pirates shared
the treasure with Cousin
Cuthbert and his friends.
They were delighted, too.

Wilbur didn't share his sardines.

Winnie AND Wilbur
UNDER THE SEA

It was holiday time for Winnie the Witch
and her big black cat, Wilbur.

'Where will we go this year, Wilbur?' asked Winnie.
She searched the internet and found a little island,
with blue sea, golden sand, and coconut trees.

The bright blue sea was full of beautiful fish.
'Don't the fish look lovely, Wilbur?' she said.
They look delicious, thought Wilbur.
'That's where we'll go,' said Winnie

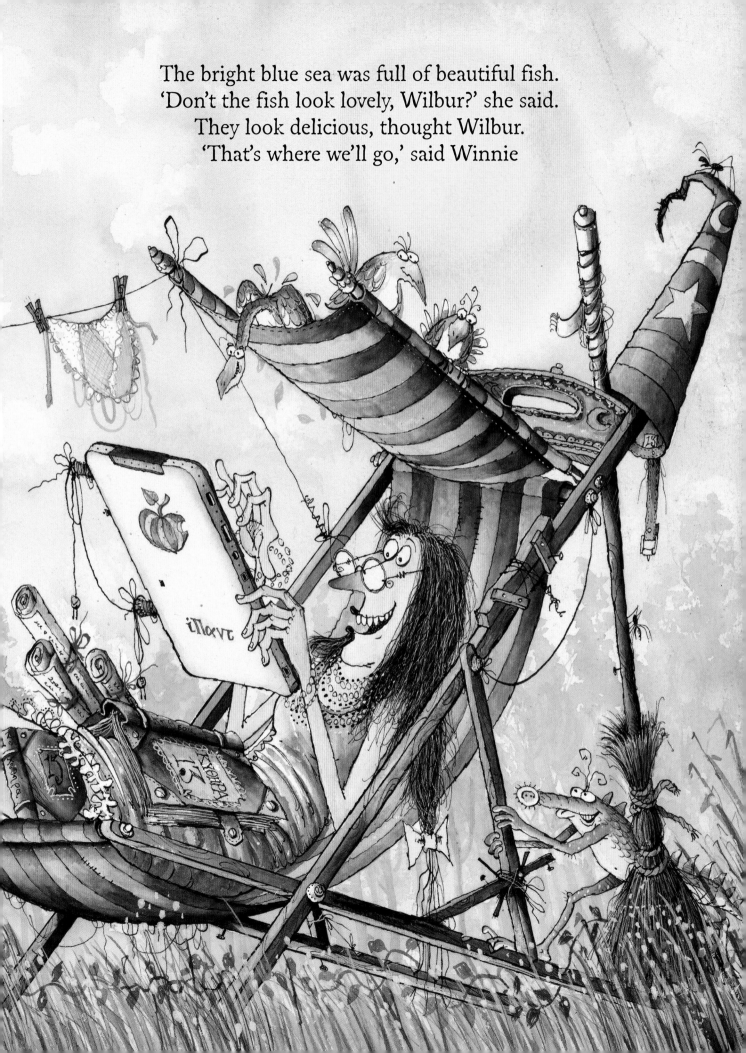

She packed her suitcase,
Wilbur jumped onto her shoulder,
and they zoomed up into the sky.

At last, there was the island.
It did look lovely.

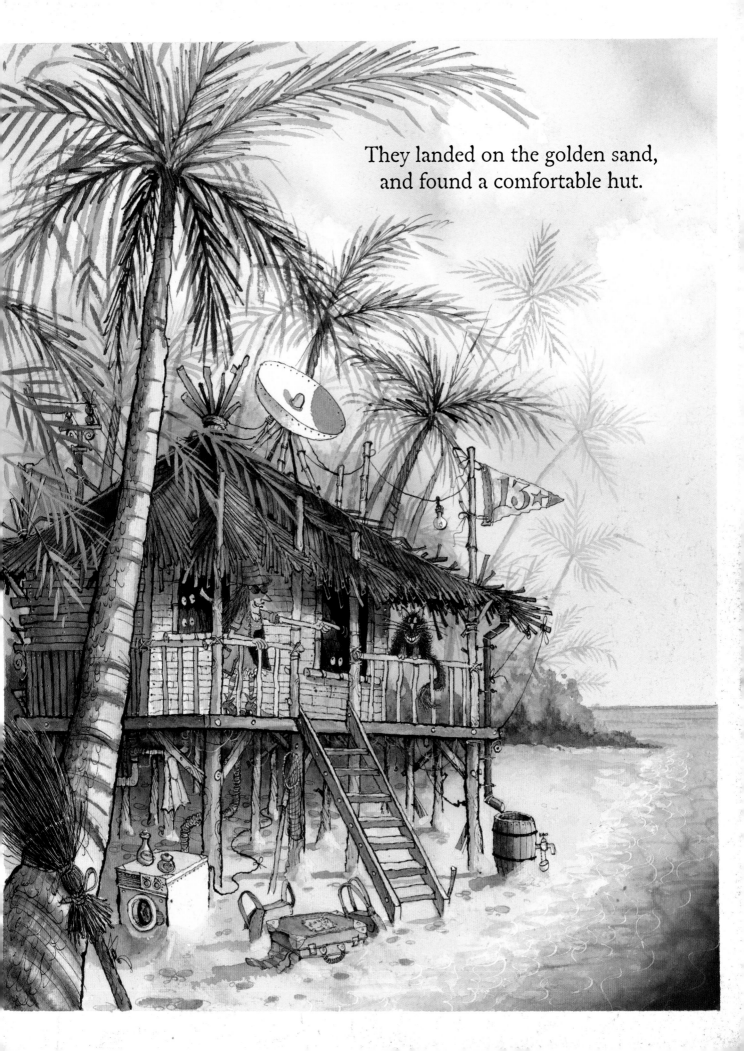

They landed on the golden sand,
and found a comfortable hut.

Winnie put on her flippers and her goggles,
and dived into the water.

Wilbur climbed a coconut tree.
That was fun.
Then he had a sleep.
That was peaceful.

Winnie was having a lovely time.
The sea was full of fish. There were
dolphins, turtles, and coral.
It was so beautiful.
Winnie wanted Wilbur
to see it, too.

'Wilbur,' called Winnie,
'come and see the fish.
You'll love them!'

Wilbur wanted to see the fish.
He put one paw in the water.
Erk! Nasty! It was wet!
'Meeeeooow!' cried Wilbur.
He hated getting wet.

GHOTI

Then Winnie had
a wonderful idea.
She waved her
magic wand, shouted,

'Abracadabra!'

and Wilbur was
no longer a cat.

He was a cat-fish!

Wilbur the cat-fish dived
into the waves and swam away.

Winnie watched him through her goggles.

He chased some tiny fish.
Then he dived under a dogfish
and played catch with a crayfish.

Wilbur the cat-fish was having so much fun,
Winnie wanted to be a fish as well.

But she couldn't be a fish.
She had to hold her magic wand.
What could she be?
Of course!

Winnie waved her wand, shouted,

'Abracadabra!'

and she was an octopus!
An octopus with orange
and yellow legs, holding
a magic wand!

It was fun being an octopus.
Winnie the octopus waved her eight legs
and floated through the seaweed,
around the coral, over the rocks.

Wilbur the cat-fish darted around her.
Thousands of fish swam with them.
Tiny fish, big fish, and, suddenly . . .

a sea lion.

The sea lion flipped its tail,
and Winnie lost her wand.

She grabbed at it, but missed.

A swordfish tried to spear it for her, but missed.

A jellyfish nearly caught it, but missed.

Down, down it sank,

into the wreck of
an old sailing ship,

and disappeared.

'Blithering broomsticks!' wailed Winnie,
but it sounded like, 'Bubble, bubble, bubble.'
'Bubble, bubble, bubble,' cried Wilbur.

They didn't want to stay under the sea for ever.
Where was the magic wand?
Stuck in the anchor? **No.**

Under the ropes? **No.**   Behind the big crab? **No.**

Wilbur flipped it out. Winnie grabbed it, waved it five times, shouted,

'Abracadabra!'

In the treasure chest? **Yes!**

and a **witch** and a **cat** floated back to the shore.

'That was exciting, Wilbur,' Winnie said.
'Too exciting. We won't do that again.
But it is beautiful under the sea.'

Then Winnie had another wonderful idea.

A little yellow boat was bobbing on the waves.
Winnie waved her magic wand, shouted,

GHOTI

'Abracadabra!'

and there, bobbing on the waves . . .

was a yellow submarine.

Winnie and Wilbur went on board.
The fish swam up to the windows and looked in.

'It is lovely under the sea, isn't it Wilbur,' said Winnie.
It's lovely and dry in here, Wilbur thought.
'Purr, purr, purr,' he said.